SURFING SHAKE-UP

BY JAKE MADDOX

text by Natasha Deen

illustrated by Katie Wood

STONE ARCH BOOKS
a capstone imprint

Published by Stone Arch Books, an imprint of Capstone
1710 Roe Crest Drive, North Mankato, Minnesota 56003
capstonepub.com

Library of Congress Cataloging-in-Publication Data
is available on the Library of Congress website.

ISBN: 9781669007111 (hardcover)
ISBN: 9781669007074 (paperback)
ISBN: 9781669007081 (ebook PDF)

Summary: Rosie loves nothing more than spending her summers
surfing while staying with her aunt Hazel in Australia. But this
summer, her cousin Flora is coming to visit, too, and Aunt Hazel
wants Rosie to teach Flora how to surf. Trouble is, Flora has a history
of being mean to Rosie—and it doesn't take long to figure out that
she hasn't changed one bit. Can Rosie set aside her hard feelings and
teach Flora how to ride some waves? Or will this shake-up to Rosie's
summer of surfing lead to a wicked wipeout?

Designer: Sarah Bennett

TABLE OF CONTENTS

CHAPTER 1

Surf's Up!

Rosie Chapman stood on the beach, dug her toes into the sand, and breathed in the ocean air. Her friends—Stella Chen, Jonah Harrison, and Camille Juma—were with her, talking about their plans for the summer. Rosie listened. Sort of.

Today was her last day of "freedom," and she wanted to surf as many waves as she could. This afternoon, she was going to the airport with Aunt Hazel to pick up Flora Nedham, Rosie's cousin. Flora was spending the next two weeks with them.

If it was any other cousin, Rosie would have been excited. But Flora? They had nothing in common. Rosie's passion was surfing. Flora's was knitting.

Actually, Rosie thought, *Flora's passion is being mean to me.*

Rosie felt a hand on her shoulder. Stella smiled at her.

"I can read your thoughts, bestie," Stella said. "Stop worrying. It's been two years since Flora visited Byron Bay, right? Maybe she's not mean anymore." She swept her arm toward the ocean. "Maybe all she wants is some Australian sea air." Stella nudged her. "You should concentrate on important things, like if we should get cake or ice cream today."

Rosie laughed. "Come on, let's go ride some waves!"

Rosie grabbed her shortboard, attached the leash to her ankle, and waded into the water. She lay stomach-down on the board and then paddled to the lineup. While keeping a safe distance between herself and the others, she watched the ocean.

When it was her turn, she spotted a swell that would break into amazing surfing waves. Rosie paddled toward it. When she got close, she turned her board toward the shore. As the wave built, Rosie paddled harder to catch it, popped up, and positioned her feet on the board.

The wave broke and pushed her toward the shore. Ocean mist sprayed her face with saltwater, and the heat of the sun warmed her back. Exhilaration thrummed through Rosie's body. Soon, she was back on the beach, out of breath and laughing.

"Let's go again!" she said when Stella rode back to the beach. Her friend nodded, and they paddled to the lineup. After they had surfed for a while, she and Stella headed to the food truck for ice cream. As she swallowed the last of her pistachio treat, Rosie spotted her Aunt Hazel.

Her aunt waved and yelled, "Time to go!"

Stella gave Rosie a tight hug. "It might not be so bad."

Rosie hoped Stella was right.

CHAPTER 2

Some Things Never Change

Rosie waited at the arrival gate, wishing she could be back on her surfboard. Just thinking about the *whoosh* of the water on the shore and the feel of the waves under her board made her feel dreamy. If only she could be there instead of waiting for Flora!

As the passengers exited, Rosie's stomach clenched. She took a deep breath.

It's been two years since Flora was here, she reminded herself. *Maybe things will be different this time.*

Flora appeared in the crowd. She was a little taller now. Her dark brown hair curled around her ears. Aunt Hazel clapped her hands in delight. She rushed over and scooped Flora into a tight hug and then waved Rosie over.

Time to ride this "wave," Rosie thought. "Hey Flora, it's nice to see you," she said.

Flora ignored her. "I'm so happy to see *you*, Aunt Hazel! I can't wait to spend time with *you*."

Rosie gritted her teeth and tried again. "Welcome to Byron Bay, Australia," she said, loud enough to startle a passerby. "It'll be fun having you around."

Flora made a show of facing her. Her eyes went wide. "Wow, is that your inside voice?" She giggled as Rosie blushed in embarrassment.

"Thanks, Posie," Flora said and then giggled again. "Oh my gosh, that's not your name. Sorry, *Rosie*."

Rosie's embarrassment turned to anger. She'd been nice and Flora had just proved she was as mean as always.

Fine, Rosie thought, *I'll do the family stuff, but no way am I hanging out with her by myself!*

"No worries, it's been a while since we've seen each other," Rosie said. "With you being here for two weeks, you'll have plenty of time to learn my name."

"About that . . . " said Aunt Hazel. "Flora's going to be here for a month!"

"A *whole month*?" Rosie stammered, eyeing her cousin.

Aunt Hazel nodded and grinned. "I wanted it to be a surprise!"

Some surprise, Rosie thought glumly.

"You're here every summer while your mom's on her archaeological digs," Aunt Hazel said to Rosie. "If the month goes well, Flora can start spending her summers here, just like you."

The idea of having to share her summer with her horrid cousin Flora made Rosie want to cry.

At least I'll be able to sneak away for surfing, she thought. *It's a sport Flora doesn't know and it'll give me a break from her.*

Aunt Hazel led the way to the baggage carousel. "The great thing about Flora being here for a month is that it'll give you plenty of time to teach her how to surf!"

Rosie stumbled to a stop and almost collided with the man behind her. "What?"

"Surfing," said Aunt Hazel. "Flora's always wanted to learn, and who better to teach her than you?"

Rosie blinked fast so no one would see her tears. How could Aunt Hazel take away her only escape from Flora?

CHAPTER 3

An Unexpected Twist

Flora's face went tight. "I want *you* to teach me, Aunt Hazel, not *her*," she whined.

Flora's pouty tone irritated Rosie, but she understood what Flora meant. Aunt Hazel used to be a professional surfer. Nowadays, she ran a surfing school. There was no better teacher than their aunt.

"I agree with Flora," said Rosie.

"I hurt my knee a few days ago," said Aunt Hazel. "It'll be another month before I can get back into the water."

Rosie's eyes narrowed. "I don't remember you hurting your knee."

"I didn't want to worry you," Aunt Hazel said, waving away Rosie's suspicion. She moved to the carousel to wait for Flora's bags.

Flora and Rosie eyed each other warily.

"There's nothing wrong with Aunt Hazel's knee," said Rosie.

Her cousin scowled. "I know that! She's forcing us to spend time together!"

"If you're so smart," Rosie shot back, "then how do we get out of this?"

"Girls!" Aunt Hazel called. "Come help me with the bags!"

Rosie didn't get a chance to talk to Flora until that night. While Aunt Hazel was watching TV, Rosie went to Flora's room.

"Any brilliant ideas?" Rosie asked.

"Not yet," said Flora. "I'm thinking!"

"I have an idea," said Rosie. "I'll teach you."

Flora's eyebrows went up. "Why?"

"The sooner we're out of each other's way, the better," said Rosie. "I'll teach you and then you can surf with Aunt Hazel."

Flora considered Rosie's words. She nodded in agreement.

"Just listen to what I tell you," Rosie said to her cousin, "and we won't have any problems."

* * *

The next morning, Aunt Hazel took them to the surf shop to rent equipment for Flora. Rosie chose a softboard for her cousin. It was orange and blue with images of fish on it.

"This board would be great for you," Rosie said.

"Why can't I have a smaller board, like the one in your bedroom?" Flora folded her arms in front of her.

"Shortboards like mine are for people who've been surfing for a while," Rosie said. "This one's good for you because you're new and need lots of help."

"Are you saying I can't learn how to surf? That I need a baby board?" Flora argued.

Rosie took a sharp breath and tried to keep the frustration out of her voice. "It's a softboard, not a baby board. It's longer, wider, and thicker, which means it'll float and give you the best chance of catching a wave. You want to surf by the end of your trip, right? Not just get dunked by the waves?"

"Rosie's right, Flora," said Aunt Hazel. "Boards like this are the best kind for learning how to surf."

Flora glared at Rosie but reached over and took the softboard.

Desperate to finish the trip, Rosie quickly helped Flora collect a wetsuit, a rash guard, and sunscreen.

That night, Aunt Hazel stopped by Rosie's room. "I know Flora gets on your nerves," she said. "But she's so excited to learn how to surf. I just thought it would be more fun for her to learn from you than an oldie like me."

Rosie almost said, *But every time I try to be nice to Flora, she ends up being mean.*

Instead, Rosie forced a smile. "I'll do a good job teaching her—just like you did for me."

Later, Rosie walked past Flora's room. Through the open door, she spotted Flora on her bed, knitting and watching surfing videos.

If Flora's actually into surfing, Rosie thought, *maybe teaching her won't be so bad.*

Then a slow, happy smile spread across Flora's face.

Surprise jolted Rosie. Flora's smile was the same one Rosie had when she watched surfing videos.

Maybe Flora and I have more in common than I realized, Rosie thought.

CHAPTER 4

Heading to the Beach

The next morning, Aunt Hazel got them up early. An uncrowded beach was better for a beginner like Flora. Plus, it meant less chance of them running into a novice surfer who hadn't learned surfing etiquette. Rosie shuddered—those surfers could be dangerous.

Rosie took a breath as she headed downstairs. Even if her cousin irritated her, it was Rosie's responsibility to make sure Flora was safe and that she understood the rules of the beach.

The girls waited in the kitchen while Aunt Hazel checked her surf app to see which beach they should visit.

"Part of being a surfer is learning to read the waves," Rosie said to Flora. "Some waves are great for beginners and some are for more advanced surfers." She leaned over Aunt Hazel's shoulder and pointed at the screen. "We'll want a sandy-bottom beach for you with soft, mushy waves. Those waves give you the best chance of catching a ride."

"She's right," said Aunt Hazel. "And a sandy bottom means you'll be less likely to get injured if you fall too."

An emotion flickered across Flora's face.

Rosie frowned. She couldn't tell what Flora was feeling. Worry churned her insides.

Will Flora start another fight? she thought.

"I know," Flora said. "I watched a bunch of surf videos last night. One recommended starting at a sandy-bottomed beach too."

Rosie breathed out in relief.

Aunt Hazel whooped. "I've got the spot for us!"

On the drive, Flora's mom phoned her. Rosie tried not to eavesdrop but she could hear them arguing.

"I know, Mom." Flora's eyes squeezed shut. "*Of course* I'm going to listen to Rosie and—Mom—I was doing surfing research, too, you know. It's not like Rosie knows everything—"

"Let me." Rosie took the phone.

Flora's eyebrows puckered with anger.

"Aunty Cassia? It's Rosie. Flora's right," said Rosie.

Her cousin's forehead smoothed out, but her eyes held a wary light.

"She's been watching videos and paying attention to everything Aunt Hazel and I say. She's going to be great at surfing." Rosie handed the phone back.

Flora looked surprised. "Thanks for sticking up for me." She returned to her call.

A thread of guilt slid along Rosie's insides. *Maybe I haven't been nice to Flora, if she's so surprised that I'd speak up for her,* she thought. *I'm going to try harder for us to be friends.*

Once they were on the beach, it was time for the surfing lessons to begin. Worry started churning in Rosie again. Surfing wasn't just about grabbing a board and jumping into the waves. Initially, Flora would spend a lot of time on the beach.

"About riding the waves—" Rosie began.

"It won't be for a while." Flora smiled. "I watched surfing videos all night. I have to learn stuff like popping up and falling before heading into the water." She crouched and drew the outline of a surfboard in the sand. "The front part is called the nose, the back part's the tail, and the sides are the rails."

"I'm really impressed!" Rosie gave her a high-five. "What else do you know?"

Flora's nose scrunched. "Not much—I fell asleep."

The girls laughed. Happiness warmed Rosie. It felt good to laugh with her cousin.

CHAPTER 5

Pop Up!

Rosie drew a vertical line in the middle of the surfboard outline. "This is the stringer," she said. "You use it to make sure you're in the middle of the board."

After Rosie drew a surfboard for herself, she showed Flora how to pop up. She lay on her belly.

"When you're looking for a wave you like," Rosie said, "your board faces the ocean. When you find one, then you turn your board to the shore."

Flora nodded.

"Paddle hard—" Rosie swung her arms along the sides of the outlined board. "When you feel the wave cresting, you pop up! Put your hands under your shoulders, lift your chest high, and then get your feet under you." Rosie demonstrated. "One foot will be back by the tail and the other will be by the middle. Keep your knees bent, but not too much, and hold your hands out for balance."

Flora's forehead wrinkled with nervousness. "Which leg goes where?"

Rosie gave her a teasing grin and a gentle push.

"Hey!" Flora stumbled forward. "Why did you do that?"

Rosie pointed at the sand. Flora's right foot was in front of her left.

"Your right foot is the dominant one," Rosie said. "It'll go by the nose. That means you're a goofy foot surfer." She lifted her left foot and shook it. "I'm a regular foot surfer. That means I lead with my left."

The girls practiced on the sand and then their boards.

"Something else we should talk about is falling," said Aunt Hazel during their break.

Rosie waxed her board and listened.

"In shallower water, it's tempting to jump off the surfboard," said Aunt Hazel, "but that's a good way to hurt your ankle or worse. If you lose your balance and you fall, try to fall on your back or your bum. The important thing to remember is making sure the surfboard isn't between you and the wave when you fall."

Aunt Hazel gestured to the ocean. "A wave has a lot of power and speed. It can push the surfboard into you." She tapped the back of her head. "And that can hurt a lot and mean a ton of stitches."

"But if there are other surfers around, then you try to keep hold of your board so it doesn't swing into them," Rosie added.

Flora's face paled. "That's a lot to remember. Maybe this was a bad idea. Maybe I should stick to knitting."

Rosie put her hand on her cousin's shoulder. "It feels like a lot because you're learning. Come on, let's catch a wave!"

CHAPTER 6

Riding the Waves

Rosie took the lead. She stood on the beach and watched the ocean for a few minutes.

"Are you reading the waves?" asked Flora.

Rosie nodded. "It's all about finding one that will let you ride for as long as possible."

"Quality over quantity," said Flora.

Rosie grinned, surprised. "You really did your homework!"

Flora blushed with pleasure.

When Rosie was sure the waves would be gentle enough for Flora, she grabbed her board.

"Make sure your leash is properly attached to your non-dominant leg and keep it behind you," Rosie said. Then she headed into the water.

Flora followed.

Rosie started paddling and then stopped when she realized Flora wasn't beside her. Rosie spun around. Flora was struggling to get her surfboard to move.

"You're nose diving," she said. "That means you're too far up on your board. Move your body back a little."

Flora shimmied backward and then paddled. Her face lit up as the board moved forward.

Rosie led them to a spot where they could watch the swells. When she spotted a good one, she yelled, "Paddle hard!" She turned her board to face the shore and then looked over her shoulder.

Flora gave her a thumbs-up.

Rosie's arms churned the water. As the wave broke, she popped up and rode to shore. She checked for Flora. Her cousin was walking out of the water carrying her board.

Aunt Hazel cheered from her spot on the beach.

"I lasted two seconds before wipeout," Flora laughed. "It was awesome! Let's go again!"

They headed back to the waves.

"Your turn," said Rosie, sitting up on her board. "Spot a wave for us."

Flora nervously twisted her fingers together.

"If it's not a good wave, I'll let you know," said Rosie.

Flora nodded. A few minutes later, she cried, "That one!"

"Perfect!" Rosie spun her board and made sure Flora was with her. "Paddle hard!"

Rosie's heart raced with excitement. The wave was under her! It crested—and she was up and riding it. She got to shore, her skin sizzling with the joy of it all.

"Nice try, Flora!" hollered Aunt Hazel.

Rosie turned.

"I didn't make the wave," Flora said to Rosie's unasked question.

They tried a third time, and Flora wiped out again.

"Why can't I get it?" She kicked the sand in frustration.

"I bet you didn't get knitting the first time you did it," said Rosie.

Flora sighed. "No, but that's different."

"No, it's not," said Rosie. "I've seen you knitting. That takes a lot of patience and attention. Surfing's the same. Let's try again. This time, I won't ride with you. I'll watch from the lineup and see if I can help you."

When they saw a good wave, Flora turned her board to shore and paddled. She popped up, rode the wave for a few seconds, and then wiped out.

"I know what's happening," Rosie said as Flora paddled toward her. "Your feet aren't in the right spot, so you can't find your balance, which causes you to fall. Try to keep your feet centered on the stringer."

Flora nodded as she headed out for another try.

Rosie chewed her bottom lip as she watched her cousin catch the wave. This time, Flora rode it back to shore. Rosie cheered and pumped her fist into the air.

Rosie caught the next wave. When she got to the beach, she ran to Flora.

"That was awesome!" Rosie said. Then she gave her cousin a high-five and a hug.

Flora's eyes shone with pleasure. "Again!"

They kept surfing until Aunt Hazel called them in. "Time to go," she said. "The beach is filling up."

"Just once more," Flora pleaded.

"Aunt Hazel's right," said Rosie. "Too many surfers can be dangerous—especially if they're new at it."

Flora's face tightened. "Just because I'm new doesn't mean I'd do anything dangerous! I've been watching the surfing videos!"

"I'm not talking about you—" Rosie started to say.

"You don't own the ocean," Flora shouted.

Anger surged through Rosie. Why did her cousin have to act like this and ruin their fun morning?

"Fine," Rosie bit out. "If you know so much—what's a turtle roll? Or a duck dive? Is dropping in a good or a bad thing?"

"Rosie, Flora, that's enough," said Aunt Hazel in her calm voice. "Flora, Rosie's right—it's your first day and it's getting crowded. Let's head home and have a proper breakfast."

On the way home, Flora turned to Rosie. "It sounded like you were taking a shot at me," she said.

"I wasn't!" protested Rosie.

"I know—I'm really sorry," said Flora. "I just . . ." she trailed off and shook her head. "Thanks for teaching me." Flora smiled and stuck out her hand. "Do over?"

"Do over," Rosie said and shook Flora's hand. She just hoped it would stick.

CHAPTER 7

Friendship Wipeout!

A week later, Rosie couldn't believe the best part of her day was hanging with Flora—in and out of the surf. Who knew her cousin was so much fun? She smiled at Flora as they set the table for breakfast.

Aunt Hazel looked Rosie's way. "I wondered if you girls might like to meet up with Rosie's friends for some surfing. Rosie, you haven't spent any time with them since Flora arrived. And Flora, your skills are getting strong."

Flora looked unsure. "Are you sure it's okay to meet your friends?"

Rosie grinned. "More than okay!" She pulled out her phone and texted them. A few seconds later, she said, "Done! They're excited to see us!"

An hour later, Aunt Hazel dropped the girls at the beach.

"This is going to be awesome," Rosie said to Flora as they hauled their boards to the beach. She couldn't wait for Stella to see that she'd made friends with Flora.

She's going to be so happy for me! Rosie thought as she spotted her friends. She and Flora headed over. "Stella, Camille, and Jonah, this is my cousin, Flora."

"Hey." Flora gave them a nervous wave.

Soon, Flora's nervousness disappeared. Too bad for Rosie, since it was replaced by her cousin's mean jokes.

Rosie watched, her heart sinking, as her cousin turned back into the argumentative, annoying person Rosie remembered. When Rosie reminded Flora to stay a safe distance from other surfers in the lineup, she rolled her eyes.

"What a worry rabbit," Flora said. "Like I'd forget!"

Rosie forced a smile. "Just thinking of your safety."

"Then you should get something for your snoring. Talk about ear safety," Flora said.

Rosie's friends laughed.

"Let's change the subject," said Rosie.

"Like to how you used to be scared of kangaroos?" asked Flora.

"You were scared of kangaroos?" asked Stella.

"That was a long time ago!" Rosie's cheeks went hot.

As Flora began to share the story, Rosie moved away from the group. She didn't want to cause a scene, but she didn't want to stay there, either. She waded into the water and paddled over to the lineup.

When it was her turn, the wave was *perfect*. Rosie popped up, leaned her rail into the water, and then pushed her weight up. The board shot to the rim. Rosie kept her body open and shifted her weight back. She carved the wave and sent a spray of water behind her board.

When she got back to the beach, her friends whooped and hollered at her epic run.

"That was amazing," said Flora.

Rosie smiled. "Thanks."

"Teach me one of those tricks," said her cousin.

Rosie shook her head. "They're advanced."

"You heard Aunt Hazel," said Flora. "She said my skills are strong."

"She said they're *getting* strong," Rosie said. "It wouldn't be safe."

"You're just saying that because you want to hog all the attention for yourself," Flora said, her voice rising.

"You're the attention hog," Rosie shouted back.

"Maybe we should do something else," said Stella.

"No," said Flora, "I came here to surf. It's not my problem if Posie is too selfish to teach me."

"That's not my name," said Rosie.

"It should be," Flora shot back. "Because you're just a poser. You pretend you're nice, but you're not!"

Rosie's anger felt like a hot rain that blistered her skin. "That's it!" She yanked her phone out of her bag and texted Aunt Hazel to pick them up.

By the time their aunt picked them up, both girls were fuming.

"She was mean and she embarrassed me in front of my friends," Rosie told Aunt Hazel that night. "I'm done trying to get along with her!"

Aunt Hazel looked sad, but she said, "I understand. Flora can hang with me."

Finally, Rosie thought, *I'm going to get a break.*

CHAPTER 8

A Change of Heart

The next day, Rosie went to the beach with her buddies. It was awesome to be with her friends again, but something was missing. Flora. Every time Rosie looked at the water, she thought of Flora's excitement and how much fun they'd been having.

Stella dropped down to the sand beside her. Reading Rosie's thoughts again, she said, "You feel bad about the fight yesterday."

Rosie nodded.

"Me too," said Stella. "All of us, actually. We love the embarrassing Rosie stories because we love everything about you." She nudged Rosie's shoulder. "But you weren't loving it and we should have seen. Sorry."

Rosie laid her head on Stella's shoulder. "Thanks. I should have just told you how I felt instead of walking away."

"Wanna catch a wave?" Stella asked.

Rosie stood and pulled Stella to her feet. A few minutes later, Rosie was riding the wave. Stella's words echoed in her ears. Maybe Flora hadn't been trying to be mean and just had a different sense of humor.

Even though I'm a better surfer and Flora's a beginner, we found a way to surf together, Rosie thought. *Maybe it's the same way with our stories. Maybe we need to find the balance between what each of us thinks is funny.*

As soon as she was back on the beach, she texted her aunt. *Flora and I need to talk. Can you come get me?*

Aunt Hazel texted back, *Of course!*

Rosie packed up and hoped she and Flora would be able to sort through their fight.

I love Flora as much as I love the waves, she thought. *I don't want to lose our friendship.*

Half an hour later, Aunt Hazel picked her up. Rosie hoped she wasn't too late.

CHAPTER 9

Always Right Rosie

When Rosie got home, Flora was waiting for her.

"I'm sorry for wrecking our day yesterday," said Flora.

"It's on me too," said Rosie. "I should have been up front about the stories being embarrassing."

Flora blushed. "I knew how you felt, but—" She took a breath. "—I didn't care."

Her words broke Rosie's heart. Flora hadn't changed at all.

"I'm so sorry!" Flora cried. "I just get so sick and tired of hearing about *Always Right Rosie*."

Rosie blinked, surprised. "What?"

Aunt Hazel set a plate of apple slices in front of them. "What do you mean, Flora?"

"My mom's always telling me I should be more like Rosie," said Flora. "Rosie's so smart and so athletic, and she's right *about everything!* It just felt good to tell the stories to show you aren't perfect." Flora shook her head. "And I felt great until I saw how much I hurt you."

"Always Right Rosie?" Rosie was mystified.

Flora nodded. "Even Aunt Hazel does it. Every time you and I disagreed, she was always like, 'Rosie's right.'" She looked at the floor. "It makes me mad . . . and jealous."

"But I'm not right about everything," Rosie said. "I just know more about surfing, that's all."

Aunt Hazel nodded. "Rosie's right—" She stopped. "Rosie makes a really good point. She knows more about surfing, and that's why I agree with her."

Tears welled up in Flora's eyes. "I'm so sorry. If you give me another chance, Rosie, I won't be mean."

Rosie nodded slowly. "How about if you teach me some knitting? I've always wanted to learn, and I bet you'll see all the ways I'm wrong!"

"Why don't you girls start on that?" said Aunt Hazel as she pulled out her phone. "I'm going to call your mom, Flora, and talk to her. It's not a great feeling, being compared to other people."

"Maybe tomorrow all three of us can go surfing," said Rosie. She looked at her aunt from the corner of her eye. "That is, if your knee is feeling better."

"You know," said Aunt Hazel, "I think it just might be healed by then."

The girls laughed and headed upstairs.

CHAPTER 10

Riding the Friendship Wave

The next morning, they headed to the beach. It was more crowded than usual.

"This is a perfect chance to watch more than the waves," Aunt Hazel said to Flora. "Pay attention to the surfers. One of the most dangerous things in the water isn't the sharks, jellyfish, or coral. It's an inexperienced surfer or an overly confident one. They make mistakes and take risks that can be a hazard to others."

While Aunt Hazel and Flora talked, Rosie watched the waves and noticed an inexperienced surfer about her age in the lineup. He was too close to the other surfers and kept stealing their waves. Making a mental note to stay away from him, Rosie paddled to the lineup.

When it was her turn, Rosie paddled to the swell. Just as she popped up and took her position, she noticed movement from the corner of her eye. It was the rookie surfer.

He dropped in front of her, stealing Rosie's wave. Irritated but unable to do anything else, Rosie let him go. Just then, the surfer panicked and dove off his surfboard. The wave kicked it toward Rosie. She tried to veer away, but the board smashed into her. It banged against her ribs and threw her off her board.

Rosie toppled under the waves. Her heart raced, but she didn't panic. She stayed under the water for a few seconds to give the surfboard time to shift away. But waves and boards were unpredictable. As she swam to the surface, she covered her head with her hands. If there was a board above her, at least her head wouldn't make first contact.

Rosie broke the surface, swam to her board, and climbed on. Just in time too! The other surfer's board was veering back at her. Rosie went flat on her belly, grabbed the rails, and duck dived under the wave and the surfboard.

When she surfaced, the surfer and his board were a safe distance from her—but not a safe distance from Flora. As he waded from the water, Rosie could hear Flora giving the surfer an earful.

"Don't you know anything about surfing etiquette?" Flora wouldn't let the surfer side-step her. "Or not being a danger to everyone around you? You're a beginning surfer—you need to respect the rules! It's rude to steal other people's waves. And you hurt my cousin!"

When Rosie got to the beach, the surfer walked up to her.

"I'm Aiden," he said, nervously rubbing the back of his neck, "I'm really sorry. The wave just looked so great. I had to try it."

"No, you didn't," snapped Rosie. "You're not a strong enough surfer and your mistake could have really injured me."

He ducked his head. "I'm sorry."

Rosie chuffed out her breath. "Just don't do it again."

Rosie turned and saw the worry on Flora's face. "I'm fine." Then she waved at her aunt. "I'm okay!"

Aunt Hazel gave a nod and glared at Aiden's back.

"You'd better stick with us," Flora said to Aiden. "My cousin will teach you everything you need to know. She's the best. Well, she's the best at everything but knitting." Flora flashed a quick grin so Rosie knew she was just teasing.

Rosie laughed. "True!" Happiness made Rosie feel light. "My cousin is smart when it comes to surfing too." She threw her arms around Flora.

"Watch what we do," Flora said to Aiden, "and learn." She gestured to their aunt. "Our aunt is an instructor. She'll help you figure it out."

Aiden sat beside Aunt Hazel as Rosie and Flora headed to the water.

"Aunt Hazel says if I want, I can visit every summer," Flora said with a nervous glance at Rosie. "What do you think?"

"I think that's a great idea." Rosie hugged her.

Flora grinned. "Come on, let's surf!"

Rosie laughed, and they ran for the waves.

About the Author

photo by Richard Jervis

Natasha Deen loves stories—exciting ones, scary ones, and especially funny ones! She lives in Edmonton, Alberta, Canada, with her family, where she spends a lot of time trying to convince her pets that she's the boss of the house.

About the Illustrator

photo by Katie Wood

Since graduating from Loughborough University School of Art and Design in 2004, Katie Wood has been a freelance illustrator. From her studio in Leicester, England, she creates bright and lively illustrations for books and magazines all over the world.

Glossary

argumentative (ar-gyoo-MEN-tuh-tive)—having a tendency to disagree with others

concentrate (KAHN-suhn-trayt)—to focus your thoughts and attention on something

crest (KREST)—the top of a wave

dominant (DOM-uh-nuhnt)—strongest or most powerful; in surfing the dominant leg is placed near the front of the surfboard

embarrassment (em-BA-ruhss-muhnt)—a feeling of shame

etiquette (ET-uh-ket)—rules that outline proper behavior

exhilaration (eg-zil-uh-RAY-shuhn)—a feeling of excitement

leash (LEESH)—a cord that connects the tail of a surfboard to a surfer's ankle

wax (WAKS)—a substance surfers rub on their boards to make them less slippery

wetsuit (WET-soot)—a piece of clothing that covers a surfer's body and provides protection from the cold, coral, and jellyfish

Discussion Questions

1. Rosie is nervous about her cousin visiting because Flora is mean to her. Do you think it would have helped if Rosie had talked to Aunt Hazel about her worries before Flora's arrival? Why?

2. One of the reasons that Aunt Hazel and Rosie take Flora surfing in the morning is to avoid crowded lineups full of inexperienced surfers. What are some ways beginner surfers can learn about surfing etiquette?

3. What types of things might Aiden learn from Aunt Hazel, Rosie, and Flora?

Writing Prompts

1. Flora watches surfing videos to prepare for her surfing lessons. Write a journal entry about how Flora might feel and what she might be thinking the night before she heads out with Rosie.

2. Imagine you're Aunt Hazel. How would you talk to Flora's mom about her comparing Flora and Rosie?

3. Rosie's surfing skills and her ability to keep calm help her get away from the danger of a surfboard being tossed by the waves. Imagine that she hadn't been able to duck dive out of the way. Write a paragraph about what might happen next.

More About Surfing!

Surfing has some unique names for its moves and equipment. Here are a few terms to help you enjoy the sport!

carve: when a surfer turns sharply at the top or the bottom of the wave; at the bottom it's called a bottom turn and at the top it's a cut back

dropping in: when a surfer cuts ahead of another surfer and steals their wave

duck dive: when a surfer holds the rails of their board and pushes themselves under a wave

lineup: the spot where waves begin to break and surfers wait for their turn to surf

pop up: when a surfer moves from lying on their stomach to standing on the surfboard

rash guard: a piece of clothing worn by surfers to protect them from the friction of lying on their boards and paddling

shortboard: a type of surfboard used by experienced surfers that is shorter, narrower, and less buoyant than a softboard

softboard: a type of surfboard used by beginner surfers; it is long, wide, and thick, allowing for the most buoyancy

turtle roll: when a surfer holds the rails of their board, flips the board upside down, and rolls as a wave washes over them